This book belongs to

_____

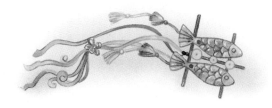

The Nightingale

BY

Hans Christian Andersen

Retold by Fiona Black

ILLUSTRATED BY

Catherine Huerta

ARIEL BOOKS

ANDREWS AND McMEEL

KANSAS CITY

Library of Congress Cataloging-in-Publication Data

Andersen, H. C. (Hans Christian), 1805–1875.
    [Nattergalen. English]
    The nightingale / Hans Christian Andersen ; illustrated by
    Catherine Huerta.
        p.   cm.
    Translation of: Nattergalen.
    "Ariel books."
    Summary: Despite being neglected by the emperor for a jewel-
    studded bird, the little nightingale revives the dying ruler with
    its beautiful song.
    ISBN 0–8362–4927–5 : $6.95
    [1. Fairy tales. 2. Nightingales—Fiction.] I. Huerta, Catherine, ill.
    II. Title.
    PZ8.A542Ni   1992
    [E]—dc20   91–40337
                                                      CIP
                                                       AC

Design: Susan Hood and Mike Hortens
Art Direction: Armand Eisen, Mike Hortens, and Julie Phillips
Art Production: Lynn Wine
Production: Julie Miller and Lisa Shadid

The Nightingale

Once long ago in China there lived an emperor. His palace was the most beautiful in the world. It was made entirely of delicate porcelain. Around the palace were huge splendid gardens full of rare plants and flowers. Beyond these gardens a great forest of stately pine trees stretched all the way to the sea. In this forest lived a little nightingale.

The nightingale sang so beautifully that no one who heard her song ever forgot it.

The poor fishermen who cast their nets in the sea all day always stopped working when they heard the nightingale sing. "How beautiful," they would sigh, forgetting their troubles as they listened to the sweet music.

Travelers came from faraway lands to visit the emperor's city. They admired the delicate porcelain palace and the beautiful gardens. But when they heard the nightingale sing, they all said, "This is the most wondrous of all."

Scholars and poets wrote books praising the emperor's palace and splendid gardens. But they praised the nightingale most of all.

These books were carried all over the world. One day the emperor himself happened to read one. "How extraordinary," he said. "This book says that of all the wonderful things in my kingdom, the nightingale is the most wonderful! But what is the nightingale? Why have I never heard of this bird?"

The emperor summoned all his ministers and courtiers and asked them about the nightingale. But none of them had heard of the bird either. Nor had any of the lords and ladies-in-waiting nor the footmen nor the cooks.

At last, one of the emperor's courtiers happened to ask a young kitchen maid about the bird.

"Oh, the nightingale!" she exclaimed. "I know her well. Every evening I go visit my old mother who lives by the sea. When I reach the forest I am always tired and sad. Then I hear the nightingale sing. Her song is so lovely that I feel as if my mother were kissing me and it makes me cry!"

The courtier was very excited when he heard this and begged the kitchen maid to take him to the nightingale at once.

So the kitchen maid, the courtier, and several of the emperor's ladies-in-waiting set out.

They had not gone far when a cow in a nearby meadow began mooing.

"That must be the nightingale now!" cried the courtier. "I have heard her song before. What power she has for such a tiny creature!"

"Oh, no!" said the kitchen maid. "That's not the nightingale! That is only a cow mooing. We have a long way to go yet."

Soon they passed a marsh where some frogs were croaking.

"So that is the nightingale!" the courtier said. "How lovely! Her voice sounds like church bells ringing."

"That is not the nightingale!" the kitchen maid laughed. "But we shall hear her soon. Look, there she is now!"

13

The kitchen maid pointed at a small brown and gray bird perched on a branch overhead. "How plain she is!" said all the ladies-in-waiting. "We never imagined the nightingale would look so . . . dull!"

Then the nightingale began to sing, and her sweet haunting melody filled the forest.

"Ah," whispered the ladies-in-waiting. "How exquisite!"

"Yes, indeed!" sighed the courtier. "Her song sounds like the tinkling of tiny glass bells!" Then he called up to the small bird, "Good day, nightingale, we have come to ask you to sing for the emperor!"

"Should I begin now?" asked the nightingale.

"Oh, no!" said the courtier. "You must present yourself at court this evening and sing for the emperor there."

"My song sounds best in the forest," the nightingale replied, "but if the emperor wishes I will come to the palace."

That evening the emperor's palace was lit with colored lanterns and decorated with silver and gold ribbons in honor of the special occasion.

In the throne room, the entire court sat gathered around the emperor. Everyone wore their finest silk robes. A gold perch had been placed by the emperor's throne for the nightingale.

At last, the little brown and gray bird flew through the open window. She took her place on the perch and began to sing.

Her song was like a bright spring day, and somehow it deeply touched everyone who heard it. The emperor bent forward to listen.

Tears came to his eyes and rolled down his cheeks.

When the nightingale was finished, the emperor said he had never heard anything so beautiful. He offered to give the bird his gold slipper to wear around her neck.

The nightingale shook her head. "I have seen tears in the eyes of the emperor," she said, "and that is reward enough."

The nightingale sang another song even more lovely than the first. Then she flew back to her home in the forest.

Everyone in the court agreed that the nightingale's singing had been a great success. Indeed, no one could speak of anything else. Some noble young ladies even tried to imitate the nightingale's song by putting water in their mouths and gurgling.

The emperor announced that the nightingale was to have a place at court. She would have a gold cage of her own and twelve servants to wait on her hand and foot.

So the nightingale sang for the court every night, and everyone raved that her song was the most wonderful in all the world.

One day the emperor received a large parcel from the emperor of Japan. This parcel had these words written on it in large gold letters: *The Nightingale*.

"This must be another book about our wonderful bird," thought the emperor as he opened the parcel. But instead, there was an artificial nightingale inside made of gold and studded with precious gems. When this nightingale was wound up, it sang like the real nightingale and bobbed its tail up and down in time to the music.

"How beautiful it is!" everyone in the court exclaimed. "Have it sing with the real nightingale, and we'll have a duet!"

So the two birds sang together but not very well. The artificial bird could only sing

the same tune over and over, while the real nightingale sang in a different way each time.

"What pretty, regular music the gold nightingale makes," said the court music master. "Most refreshing." The courtiers all agreed and insisted that the artificial nightingale be allowed to sing alone.

So the gold nightingale sang. The entire court said that it sang as well as the real bird. "It's so much prettier to look at, too!" they whispered, admiring the golden bird's sparkling wings. So they wound it up, and it sang the same song thirty-three times in a row. They would have happily listened to it again, too, when the emperor declared that the real nightingale must be allowed to sing.

The courtiers looked for the real nightingale, but she was gone. She had flown out the window and back to her home in the forest. "Such an ungrateful bird!" sniffed the courtiers. "But never mind. We have the best nightingale right here!"

After that the real nightingale was banished from the kingdom. Then the artificial bird was put in a gold cage beside the emperor's throne. Every evening the court gathered to hear it sing.

A year passed. The gold nightingale sang every night. Everyone knew its song by heart. But this made them like it all the more since they could all sing along. Then

one evening the emperor wound up the gold nightingale as usual. But instead of singing, it made a strange whirring noise. The gold nightingale was broken!

The emperor called to him all the kingdom's best watchmakers. They examined the bird carefully and tinkered with its insides until they managed to make it work again. But the bird's springs were worn out. The watchmakers told the emperor the gold nightingale could sing only once a year at the most. This made everyone at the court very sad.

Five years passed and a worse grief fell upon the kingdom. The emperor grew ill and seemed certain to die. His people, who loved their emperor, were truly sorry and it seemed that there was nothing they could do.

The emperor lay in his royal bedroom. He was so still and pale that everyone in the court believed he would die at any moment. All the lords and ladies-in-waiting acted as though he were already dead and hurried to pay their respects to his successor.

Meanwhile the emperor lay all alone in his splendid bedroom.

He lay on his cold golden bed with the silent golden nightingale beside him in its golden cage.

The emperor could hardly breathe. He felt as if there were a great weight on his chest. He opened his eyes and saw Death sitting beside his bed, wearing the emperor's golden crown.

Strange faces appeared around the bed and spoke to the emperor. Some were kind faces, but some were terrible and cruel. They were all the emperor's past deeds—good and bad—come to haunt him now that Death was so close.

"Do you remember?" they whispered in the emperor's ear, making him toss and turn.

"If only I could hear some music," the emperor moaned, "then I would not have to listen to these voices." He turned to the golden nightingale beside him. "Please sing for me," he pleaded. "I have given you a gold cage and my own gold slipper to wear around your neck. Now, I beg you, please sing to me so I might hear some music before I die!"

But the golden nightingale remained still. There was no one to wind it up and make it produce a single note.

The room seemed very quiet and cold. Death drew closer and stared with his great hollow eyes at the emperor.

Suddenly, a burst of sweet music came through the open window.

It was the real nightingale. She had heard how ill the emperor was and had come to sing to him.

The nightingale sang of spring when new green leaves uncurl on the trees and colorful fragrant flowers bloom. The emperor felt his blood begin to flow more quickly. Color came to his face and he sat up to listen. Even cold Death was pleased and begged, "Sing on, nightingale!"

So the nightingale sang of peaceful churchyards where pale roses grow and of quiet streams where willow trees weep. As she sang Death grew weary and longed to sleep in the quiet chill of his own garden. At last, with a sigh, he slipped out the window.

The emperor felt strong and well again and cried, "How can I ever thank you, nightingale? I sent you from my kingdom, yet you sang for me and saved my life. Ask me for anything and you shall have it."

"You wept the first time I sang for you," said the nightingale. "And that is reward enough. Now let me come to your window each night and sing for you. I will sing of happy things and sad ones, too. From my song you will learn of all that happens in your kingdom. Only never let anyone know it is a little bird who tells you!"

"Very well," said the emperor. Then the nightingale sang for him again, and the emperor fell into a deep refreshing sleep.

The next morning, when the sun rose, the emperor's servants came in expecting to find him dead. Imagine their surprise when he came walking toward them instead and wished them all a good morning!